The Lake Boy

NewCon Press Novellas

Set 1: *(Cover art by Chris Moore)*
    The Iron Tactician – Alastair Reynolds
    At the Speed of Light – Simon Morden
    The Enclave – Anne Charnock
    The Memoirist – Neil Williamson

Set 2: *(Cover art by Vincent Sammy)*
    Sherlock Holmes: Case of the Bedevilled Poet – Simon Clark
    Cottingley – Alison Littlewood
    The Body in the Woods – Sarah Lotz
    The Wind – Jay Caselberg

Set 3: The Martian Quartet *(Cover art by Jim Burns)*
    The Martian Job – Jaine Fenn
    Sherlock Holmes: The Martian Simulacra – Eric Brown
    Phosphorous: A Winterstrike Story – Liz Williams
    The Greatest Story Ever Told – Una McCormack

Set 3: Strange Tales *(Cover art by Ben Baldwin)*
    Ghost Frequencies – Gary Gibson
    The Lake Boy – Adam Roberts
    Matryoshka – Ricardo Pinto
    The Land of Somewhere Safe – Gary Gibson

The Lake Boy

Adam Roberts

NewCon Press
England

First published in the UK by NewCon Press
41 Wheatsheaf Road, Alconbury Weston, Cambs, PE28 4LF
July 2018

NCP 161 (limited edition hardback)
NCP 162 (softback)

10 9 8 7 6 5 4 3 2 1

ISBN:

978-1-910935-85-9 (hardback)
978-1-910935-86-6 (softback)

Cover art by Ben Baldwin
Cover layout by Ian Whates

Minor Editorial meddling by Ian Whates
Book layout by Storm Constantine

One

January 31st [1795]:

The hill-streams mark the great slope with lines like tiger stripes, if that animal's colouration were *green* and *silver* instead of orange and black. Lines so regular they seem designed, the work of mankind, and not the flow from Mater Natura herself. The sheep are congregated together upon the great hill, tho none but the wind be their preacher. They bow their heads, as we ours in church. They kiss the grass. I have the fancy the grass is a specie of hair, over which the wind works like a brush; and this in turn set another fancy into my brain, that this was the hair of the divine goddess. Did not Mary wash the feet of Our Lord with her own hair? Are sheep not his animals? Indeed, are they not Him, Himself? And so, I bethought me, they kiss, in reverence. I shared this fancy with my brother, and he looked concernedly and severe upon me – a look I had not seen since before Christmas. 'A strange maggot,' he said, 'such as I hoped you had grown beyond. Repress it, Cynthia my love, or it is like to run loose in your head. Have a care, dear sister,' he said, and straightened himself as I have seen him do a hundred times in the pulpit – drawing his preacherly dignity upon himself, to impress the seriousness upon him. I bowed my head, a sheep myself, and agreed with him.

We completed our walk and took tea – the last of the batch, and Monday we must go along the road to Alfield and buy more if we wish it again.

'Perhaps we should do without,' said George. 'As a discipline – God calls us to renounce, does he not? And it *is* an expense.'

But in my heart, O brother, I thought: what God calls us to renounce *is* renunciation! God is the everlasting yea, not a black sun of no & no & no. I said nothing of that, of course. At home I took out my notebook upon the pretence of sorting my *notae sermoni*, but in truth to look again at the copy I have made of the poem of the *The Tyger*, which I bought as a small sheet, coloured most fine, when we lived in Clarkenwell. I wept at the beauty of the sentiment and force in this little lyric, and must stuff the bolster in my mouth lest G. hear me and grow concerned, for the house is so small and there are slits between the floorboards through which the slightest whisper falls like running water into the room below.

February 22nd:

Die sabbati requies est. Church three quarters full, George in good voice, coughing but little, and clearing his throat after every sentence. The weather had slipped a little, from Saturday's brightness, and a sleet the colour of lard was falling from the sky. But George held fast to his intention to preach his first spring sermon, and so he chose the verse *For, lo, the winter is past, the rain is over and gone, the flowers appear on the earth, the time of the singing of birds is come, and the voice of the turtle dove is heard in our land; the fig tree puts forth her green figs, and the vines with the tender grapes give a good smell. Arise, my love, my fair one, and come away.* I grew over-excited, I confess it, and was compelled to unpin my brooch and press the point into the heel of my hand to stop me from crying out in joy. Yet such *life* there is, in Solomon's Song – such vivacity of physical sweetness. Tho I was in church, yet I am shamed that I pushed my reticule under my hindquarters and took the ecstasy of Saint Theresa as G. preached, and saw her lovely face in my soul's vision at the moment of most sweetness. I do not think the other congregants observed me in this, or if they did perhap they suspected me only of a secret ranter enthusiasm in my worship. At any rate, most of the congregants, being unused to Graham as a preacher, distracted by his coughing hardly observed me at all.

G.'s theme of the sermon was *The things which are seen are types of the things which are not seen. The works of creation are pictures to the children of God of the secret mysteries of grace.* That evening I took notes upon his own manuscript, as ever, and filed it with the select. Tomorrow I shall go to Alfield to buy tea (not trusting Molly with the commission) and shall call upon Mr. Hebblethwaite the Printer too, to urge him with such will as I possess to the task, that the world be given the chance to read my brother's holy words.

There was a strange thing in church, after the hall was emptied and G. stood to bid each soul farewell at the archway – they pausing not to converse, but dashing through the downpour to their carriages, or along the lanes to their homes – I, returning inside to fetch my reticule, saw a figure by the altar staring at the glass above. I bethought me it was Old Harry, who serves the church as churchwarden tho he's so old and so near to stone-blind that G. must do the labour. But Harry is a man and this figure a boy of slender frame, and clad not in Sunday cloathes, but poor gear indeed.

It is a fine piece of work, the window: clear glass at the edges but a fine red and green portrayal of Saint Richard Rolle in the middest, and the boy was absorbed in it. I was not angry, *in truth not*, to see the urchin there, but puzzled as to how he came in, for I had not noticed him in the service, and he had not passed the main door as G. and I stood there. He might, I supposed, have come in at the back. He looked at me, and there was loveliness in his face, for all that he was ragged. But then I looked again, and saw that in fact his face was puckered and scarred on the left side, as if he had been burned with a brand. I recoiled to see this, but he maintained his smile.

'It is a fine likeness,' he said, in a voice like a girl's.

'How came you here?' I demanded of him, with more asperity than I intended. Say but that I was surprised.

'How we all come, by God's structuring grace,' he said. I recall this phrase exactly, for that it was so odd, and so odd to hear from a young boy's mouth. For who talks of *structuring* grace? I have never come upon the phrase, least of all from so young a one. His speech was neither Cumberland not Lancashire, but came upon my ears as London, if anything. 'Mistress,' he said, meeting my gaze, 'only affirm.' The clouds parted and sunlight came through like a highway of brightness and the red of Saint Richard's tunic became the full wine-glass with a candle behind it, and the green of Saint Richard's tunic became like the emerald ice of deepest December when the brumal winter light glitters on it. The clouds closed again and dullness became the quality of the light once more.

'Begone,' I said, afeared.

'I am the boy, neglected and abused,' he said; 'and I am Saint Peter, who holds the door open for you.'

I put my face in my hands, tho only for a moment. Yet when I looked again he was not there. Sleet shuddered upon the glass. There was but one way out of the church save the front door, and, being startled, I chased down to it: through the vestry and to the side door. It was locked with the key inside the lock (which was just like Harry's carelessness) so I deduced the boy had gone out that way; but when I strove to turn the key it was so stiff as to shriek like a kicked dog. It took both my arms full labour to turn, and I would swear it had not been beyond the strength of a child – besides, the noise it made, unoyled, and the time it took me. Then the door, which is massy wood, took my shoulder to swing. The view is over the little churchyard, and so across Blaswater itself, smoaked and shrouded in sleet. I could not see where the boy had gone.

I say no more of the prickly sense it gave me in my *plexus solaris*, or how the hairs on my head trembled as 'twere with electricity at the encounter, for as G. says, I must learn to read such symptoms in the body for what they are, precursors to my mental disarrangement, and so to be stifled at once. I did not mention the boy to G.

A famous astronomer has come to stay in the village: but I did not catch his name.[1] There are strange doings in the skies, it seems! – and he hopes to see them.

Monday.

Hard rain all day, too wet to journey out. I worked at my text of the *Liber de secretis naturae*; I have reached the fourth section. G. again urged me to some apostolic or patristic work, but the Church Fathers are all translated already, and what more would I bring?

I asked Molly the name of the boy with the burned face, but she claimed there was none such who lived in the locality. Surely so remarkable a thing, as a half-burned visage, would be remembered! Could he have come from further away?

---

[1] [**marginalium**: *Mr Powser, from Greenwich*]

Tuesday.

Mr Withers called, and at his insistence accompanied me to Alfield. Went up the pallade and over the tops of the hills, till we came by Mr W.'s direction to a new and very delicious pathway, which conducted us to the summit. Sat a while upon the high heath, Mr W. upon a flat rock, me with my legs crosst beneath my skirts. How the whole hill did seem alive! – its skin restless and glittering with the motion of the short grass in the wind, and the spiders' webs thick-woven as cloth, some flapping as flags in the air. Far below was Blaswater Lake, with mist still upon it, as muslin. At the heighth of the hill I stood in my toe's ends, and saw sunlight upon the land, and a miles' slope of grass shimmering, and the insects passing.

The path down took us past certain oaks that grow on the further ridge, whose bark is grey as granite. The shafts of the trees show the columns of a Gothick ruin. At no point did Mr W.'s speech exceed the bounds of mildest courtesy, and I reassure myself that G. is mistaken concerning his intent. G.'s worrit will grow as the date for M.'s arrival approaches, of course; for he hopes to see me settled – tho (for him) it is but clutching straws, and (for me) the narrow escape.

At Alfield: Mr Heb. the Printer neither at home nor his shop (in Burnside); Bohea tea was 3/- a pound, a full threepenny dearer than before; the shopkeeper spoke some blather concerning the war to explain. I paid, withal, for I know G. likes his tea, for all that he urges us to forego it.

The gossip in the street is of strange stars, like Magi beacons, seen over Blaswater. I for one have seen none such.

G's cough worse today.

2nd March (Mon).

Went to Harrison's for a late supper. We discussed the

likelihood of the Franks intervening in the new-declared Batavian Republic, and I may flatter myself that I contributed good sense to the discussion. Retired to closet to relieve my waters, and wept for some minutes, but returned to company in good chear. God save me from the sin of pride.

Returning home with G. and Mr. Stark, whose way lay with ours a mile or more, there was cloud in the sky like the finest Lebanon gauze thro which the moon shone with a light like white milk poured, and all the earth was chessboarded with shadows and silver. There came a moment of peculiar splendour, when the clouds were cloven asunder as (it seemed) by the sheer force of the lunar light, and left the moon at the apex of a black-blue vault. She processed in regal form, attended by myriads of courtly stars, tiny, and bright, and pin-sharp. The fire was out upon our return, and G. scolded Molly, but I was tyred and went upstairs. Here, with no bed-warming-pan, I was compelled to writhe under the covers to heat the cloathes of the bed, and this action grew as the sheets twisted between my thighs, and so the moonlight bathed me through to my soul, and I saw the lustrous face of the White Goddess of the Moon, and bethought me almost to feel the softness of her white bosom pressing against me, and the tenderness of her kisses, and so I passed into that brief trance of bliss. But as soon as after I felt the mortification of shame pour through my innards, for when I rested again, my breath short, I heard silence below me, and then the resumption of low voices as G. rebuked Molly for letting the fire die. I fear they heard me at my serpentine writhing in the bed, and were shocked to silence, only resuming later. The vexation of shame almost brought me to tears – yet the morn (as I write this) G looked only kindly upon me over breakfast. His cough seems much improved.

4ᵗʰ March.

I saw him again, on the Hattonhill road. He smiled at me, with a man's smile tho he be but a child – if he be that. Smiling made the scars upon his face pucker and gurn, in a most disagreeable fashion. When I came over to him to ask his name he was not there.

8ᵗʰ M.

Die sabbati requies est. G. managed almost all of his sermon without coughing, which he afterwards ascribed to God's mercy.

10ᵗʰ March.

Mr Withers called on us at breakfast, on his way to the Estate of Sir Harald, where he has business, and along too came his aunt Elizabeth – yet, tho she be his aunt she cannot be more than four or five years his senior, so I must assume she be the younger of his grandparents' children. She is a well favoured woman, only a little taller than I, but broader and more buxom; her face is clear white complexion, with a nose perhaps too long and sharp to be accounted handsome, yet with light expressive eyes and a sweet mouth. Her hair is dark umber, and her neck long – perhaps her loveliest feature. She is married to a tax collector in Broughton West, with whom she has two sons; the boys at school, and when they are away she often stays (she says) with her nephew in Alfield, for she does not like the sea air. She seemed to me altogether a charming and amiable woman, and I was pleased that she embraced me upon departing – tho we had but met – so much so, in truth, that I wept, and could not stop weeping after they had gone, which caused George to rebuke me, and with good cause.

I took to my bed the afternoon, and chastised myself, and marked again the *via appia sanguina* upon the inside of my arm with the pin of my brooch. My thought was aye and still of the pressure of Mrs Elizabeth's breast upon my own as she embraced me, and where she has only purity and decency about her, I could not prevent the heat in my lap at the thought. Up and down the brooch pin marched, and I only stopped because the blood became to run clear and I feared to sully the bedcloathes. O, disgusting, I am!

11th.

Up early. A thick fog obscured the prospect, but from the front door the church was a square shape, and the nearer trees; beyond was opaque, until ten by the hallclock, when the whiteness thinned and the mist could be seen as moving. Exquisitely beautiful in its purity. I walked until my shawl was sopping. The mist passed upon the sheep and over them and it seemed to me that it possessed more of life than those quiet creatures, whose only thought was to chew the grass. The unseen birds singing in the mist. The dampness doth not conduce to good breathing in my brother's bronchitis.

14th March.

A Saturday. I completed the fifth section of *Liber de secretis naturae*. I regret, somewhat, casting the English as blank verse. How far my numbers fall short of Shakspere and Milton!

In the afternoon a strange thing: I sent Molly out to shoo sheep from the graveyard, tho she scowled at me at the commission – but I had the strange intimation these innocent creatures were sucking up the substance of the dead bodies

13

beneath, as through straws. So I stood at the window and watched the girl push the sheep away and chase them, and I felt my brother come close behind me, and lay a hand upon my shoulder. Oh, but then I saw George outside, walking up along the lane, and recalled that he had gone to call on a parishioner.

The breath in my own lungs became as winter mist. The light dimmed. I could feel aye the pressure of the arm, and yet I was in too great a terror to turn and confront my companion. There was a shudder in my hands that would not leave me be. G. came up the path and saw me at the window and smiled, and passed, and all through this the pressure of the hand was on my shoulder – more, in sooth, as if a finger or thumb were pressed into the central point of the blade of my shoulder. And then the sound of the latch turning, and the groan of the door as it opes, and I turned in a panic to cry out to my brother – but there was nobody there, and I was alone in the parlour.

17th March.

Letter from Mr. Bubner, the Printer, in London town, declining my verses for publication, which fact occasioned the despondency in my soul whose true cause is wicked pride, and which I have yet to mortify out of myself. Yet did he agree to passing over the poem on the soul to Mr. W. H., and commended them to at least magazine appearance:

> *Mid the rich store of nature's gifts to man*
> *Each has his loves, close wedded to his soul*
> *By fine association's golden links.*
> *As the Great Spirit bids creation teem*
> *With conscious being and intelligence,*
> *So man, his miniature resemblance, gives*

To matter's every form a speaking soul,
An emanation from his spirit's fount,
The impress true of its peculiar seal.
Here finds he thy best image, sympathy.

In a post scriptum he rebuked me, with fair enough show of courtesy, for obscuring my gender from him during our initial correspondence, such that he only found it out soon before writing to me. I feel the dreadful mendacity of this more pressingly than I did before. In the afternoon I wept so that my shift became wet withal.

22nd March

Die sabbati requies est. Mr. W and his aunt, Mrs Eliza Jones, came early to attend church; and she to bid farewell for a time, for she was returning to the west for some weeks the morrow morn. It was gracious in her.

G. preached on John 8:48-59, and his theme was *Death is not Known in the Life with Christ.* At the portion where the Jews say unto him, Thou art not yet fifty years old, and hast thou seen Abraham? And Jesus replies, Verily, verily, I say unto you, Before Abraham was, I am. And took they up stones to cast at him: but Jesus hid himself, and went out of the temple, going through the midst of them, and so passed by – I wept. After the service Eliza took my arm and walked with me.

So solicitous she was that I confessed all my recent disorder of the mind, and admitted to seeing a ghost, or spirit, or devil, or what it might be. I confessed further that my brother was concerned for the wellbeing of my mind – and told her (poor lady! She had hardly asked for so much) of my time in Clare House under restraint, and of the sorrow of my parents at my erratic behaviour, and at the way a high and giddy soul would take possession of me. In all this she comforted me, and we walked the length of Blaswater fell, and then, it being sunny, to the top of Brandreth Hill, where we were alone save one old woman gathering furze. We sat together, and she consoled me further, and embraced me, and I wept in sheer relief. 'Do not be hasty to condemn your senses,' she advised. 'Do you not know this land is rich in stories and witches and ghosts? Blaswater is the deepest lake in the district, and who knows how many bodies it has claimed? Some say their spirits wander the shore.'

I laughed at this, and so she, and with great delicacy she thus restored the good mood. We came home, pausing in a copse to embrace, with loving kindness, and my heart sang like a bird. The sun set that day in robin redbreast colours, and I wept with happiness to have found so true a friend. How clever her fingers! How solicitous of my happiness. How sorry I shall be to be denied her company for the months to come.

23rd March

Monday. A grey, sad day; I barely able to rowse myself, and no work done upon my Latin. I mark this day with a black stone.

26th

On this day I saw again the ghostly boy, loitering in the churchyard between the vicarage and the church. I, being full of fury for reasons that are beyond my ken, came flying from the front door to rebuke him. I found him not there, but, looking back at the house, saw him at the upstairs window, he the while gazing down upon me with a strange expression upon his ruined countenance. A cold drizzle began, like ocean spray after a great wave, say, has broken on the seawall, soft and falling slow, yet very chill. The door had shut behind me and was stiff with the damp weather, and I wept in vexation as I hauled and battered it, until Molly came down in a fright thinking me a robber and called through the wood that she would send for a constable – as if we lived still in London, the foolish hen! I, crying betimes, gathered myself and after some importuning persuaded her to open the door (which she, in her panic, had locked), and so I came in wet as a bather, and rushed upstairs – but my room, of course empty, mocked me, and on returning down I slipped and bruised my back leg blue in the fall.

27th

George received certain letters today. From one he read aloud news of the British Army evacuated from Bremen in the Flanders Campaign, under the command of the Duke of York, and the ill news this be for his friend Samuel Pettison, who has gone thither to spread the minister to all Anglicans caught up in the war. After this thought, as I rose to assist Molly with the dinner, he added, as if it were an unimportant post-script, that Miss. Bainbridge will visit in a fortnight. He thought I daresay to avoid my vexation with this incidental telling, yet was I vexed, and wept. 'Where will she stay? Not here, there is not room enough a cottage for the likes of her!' George, growing angry after the restrained manner of his character, sent Molly out of the house on some pretext and took down the crop he had stored above the sideboard. He bade me remember our father's dying instruction, that he not spare the rod with me when I flew into one of my insanities, and requested in a low voice whether chastisement was needful on this occasion? I stretched myself on the boards, weeping full, and clutched his ancles and begged him no, no – and he wept too, then, for his heart is not hard. He kept clearing his throat with that specially resonant sound he makes when most sad. He has never struck me since our father passed, and I do not know if he has the mettle so to do. Then he raised me up and embraced me and spoke more kindly words to me: as, would I spoyl his chances with Miss Bane (as I call her, secretly) for marriage and the funds it would bring? Would I truly wish to remain here, in this faraway place, and deny him preferment in the Church, and a life again in the South? I, of course, cried no, and no, and no – but my wicked heart was calling *yea*! – for I bethought me of Eliza, Eliza, and wanted to be with her, tho it be in the glitter-freeze of the northern pole!

Molly returned, poking her nose in like a mouse, and I looked as dignified as I might. I spent an hour working at one single sentence of moderate Latin, and my breast was a tempest within.

29th

I have neglected to set down the occurrences of this week that follows, so I do not recollect how we disposed of ourselves to-day.

5th **[April]**.

Sabbath.

6th.

I do not remember this day.

7th.

A cold and blustery morning. I walked half of the way along Blaswater shore, and watched the motion of the waves. There is a quality to the surface of the waters like hammered pewter, and the grey is *glaucos*, which is to say, it hath blue and green within aye a metallic sheen, and something divine too. The tiger's eye is reputed amber in colour, yet Eliza's eye is blue-grey as the Goddess Athena, and she the truer tiger.

A little boat upon the turbid water, and a boy within it, fishing – tho too distant for me to see if it be he.

9th.

Basil is our guest for two nights, and sleeping toe-to-head in G.'s bed for want of space. He, G. and I walked to the hill-tops, a very cold bleak day. We were mocked on our return by a severe hailstorm. Basil recited Shakspere for us after supper, and the words brought sorrow beautifully out of my soul. I wept, which he took a great sign of favour.

10th

The News from London is of the marriage of the Prince of Wales.

11th.

I have no memory of this day.

13th.

I look over this diary and find I can remember nothing of the fortnight, save the image of the boy in the rowing boat upon the turbid waters, and that I thought a dream. Or did I see it, true? I weep often. George appears as the hallclock chimes, with hourly regularity, and his face a painted picture of concern. I assure him things are well.

16th.

Walked I know not where.

18th A[pril].

No memory of this day.

April 23rd.

Walked by the thin light of the horned moon. A comet in the sky over Glinster Coombe, a blurred dot of light with a pigtail of white drawn behind it. My heart was filled with sweetness, and sweetness in my soul, at the sight. I watched it, and then in an instant of purest wonder, I bethought myself that the comet was coming down to earth, to nestle yea in the valley of Blaswater itself! But the light was a lantern, and it bobbed out along the road; and then it was George, and Old Harold who is lay warden for the church. They had been searching me, and George wrapped me in his cloak, and together they led me to the house.

24th

George brought me tea for breakfast, which I drank with a good will.

Strange lights in the skies again, this night.

25th

I have not seen the scarred boy in a week, and this after a time (I do believe) when I saw him every day.

26th **Sunday**.

My first attendance at church for some time. Several congregants solicitous for my health. G. has put it about that I have had a fever, which is not the truth. How it pains him to utter even the whitest of lies!

Two

27th Monday.

George about on parish business the morn, and returning at noon hungry – for he rose before dawn, and omitted to break his fast. His face very grim, and his cough worse than usual. We sit quiet and eat some bread and cheese together, he with a glass of old wine sweetened from its sourness with sugar, and I with small beer. 'Where is Molly?' I asked him, in innocency and he looked very severe upon me, so that I quailed.

So we talk, and he tells me: Molly has returned over the hills to her father's farm. And the cause is me, for (he says) I approached her in a manner gross, and she fled from the vicarage. I have no memory of this. 'When I confronted you,' George says, 'you begged forgiveness upon the holy sepulchre, and I granted it, insofar as it is in my humble power as a sinner to do so. You swore you had put all such unnaturalness behind you. You swore,' he meeting my gaze very hard, 'upon the Bible.' This the Bible our mother clutched to her breast as she died; so my oath was solemn indeed.

I nodded at this: 'the memory was so ill,' I told him, 'that my mind has repelled it, and given it no house in my skull. I am heartily sorry, brother, for my behaviour, and I shall remedy myself I promise.'

'You have had,' he says, not now able to meet my gaze, 'a

relapse, dear sister.'

'I fear so. But with God's help it shall be the last!'

'I have been in communication with an honest fellow called Magnoble, who keeps a house in Yorkshire that –' But this I did not wish to hear, for I knew the meaning of it well enough, and recalled my time before in the London asylum, it being no experience I wish ever to repeat. So I wept and embraced him and begged him say no more for I would be good.

Then, at George's instigation, we prayed together, on our knees right there in the parlour. And my heart was lightened. When I asked who shall be our maid-of-all-works, he told me that old Mrs Gill, the widow, was filling that role, yet not sleeping in the stair cubby but making her way over from Hattonhill, and so not in the house every day.

Then he told me sad news: a young boy had, it seemed, drowned in Blaswater lake. At this my heart quailed within me, so I asked for the story, and looking sideways at mine reaction to ensure I was not permitting the news to upset me, told me the story. He was an orphan boy, who lived, it is said, with Farmer Mawbeer, a surly fellow who does not attend church. There are stories of his farm, said G., for he keeps a number of boys there to work the fields, and all are orphans. 'For all we know,' said George, 'he works from Christian Charity and the noblest motives, for who but God knows everyone's heart? Still, the gossip in the alleys is that he is a slaver and beats the boys, feeds them gruel and makes them work all the hours, even on the Sabbath day – for, according to the report of Farmer Smithson, over Hattonstreather way, this Mawbeer insists on working that day as any other. *The beasts need tending that day as all through the week*, he says, *and an idle Sunday is an indulgence only the wealthy can afford.* George shook his head. 'Perhaps the fellow is a heathen. At any rate, the boy is supposed to have run off, and several people saw him by the lake, and then Mrs Granstone said she saw him run, as if pursued by hounds, straight at the water. She said there were lights after him – perhaps Mawbeer was pursuing him, with a lantern.'

'It was dark, then?' I asked.

'I believe it so – dusk, tho perhaps no dark night. Mrs Grastone's account is not clear, for you know what a muddlemind she is. She says the lights flew in the sky. She says the boy swam so well, hard t'ward the middest of the lake, it seemed he walked upon the water.'

'Like Christ!' I said; but the scowl with which G. greeted this blasphemous comparison silenced me.

'But on this point she is adamant,' he went on. 'That the lad ran to the lake, and afterward he swam. Perhaps he hoped to reach the far side, altho why swim the breadth and not walk around, I know not. A ragged boy, underfed, unused to swimming – and plunging into the cold waters after sunset? Blaswater has swallowed him, I fear.'

'What was his name?' I asked.

George did not know. 'Tom, I think. Or so someone told me. Unless I imagined it? Or Tom be a generic?'

So much speechifying provoked his cough, and he racked his throat and chest so much that he was compelled to lie down for a while. When he did this, I walked alongside the palings and up to the peak of the Coombe, to clear my head. The poor plight of the boy was sorrowful; but he could hardly have been a ghost *before* he drowned! Perhaps the boy was in the habit of running off, and this was the apparition I had seen, so many times – tho that hardly answered to most of the times I had seen him. If it be a ghost, I said to myself, it must be the ghost of some other boy; and in sooth there was no shortage of orphan boys, what with the war and the hard harvests.

May 3rd

Die sabbati requies est

4th

Mr Withers called, to assure himself (he said) of my return to
health. But he stayed so long, and drank two brews of tea, and
chattered so gabblingly of the news – there are fears the
Prussians will again carve Poland into portions, and the talk in
London is of the volume *Poetical Sketches*, by Miss Anne Batten
Cristall, which perchance he mentioned only to encourage me
in my ambitions (I know not, nor of her). We talked also of the
sad news of the drowned boy, that I began to suspect his
earnestness had something of a romantic kind to it. Perhaps I
misconceive. I bethought myself of how far he falls below his
aunt in comeliness.

A little after eleven Mrs Gill came in, and at this like a
hare young Withers was startled away, bowing before me like a
Prussian himself, with his heels together, and announcing
himself inexpressibly delighted that I was returned to health,
and in such bloom. I saw him to the door, and for the first
time took a true look at him – medium height, complexion a
little dark, and with the dots of his stubble black as soot, like
smuts on a leaf. His hair is lustrous, and there is a sweetness in
the shape of his eyes, but I think his only because they remind
me, I fear, of his aunt. As he left he dropt the remark (as if it
the least significant matter in the world!) that Eliza was again
stopping with him, and I had to hold myself from running
after him begging him to give her my dearest good wish and
begging her to call.

I walked in the wood after, my heart full of strange joy.
The place was rich in flowers, and I was sorry not to know

their names – a beautiful palish golden flower, thick and round in the body, the petals doubled, very sugared in its smell; another bloom I recognised as cranesbill, like little clasps of imperial purple; the grassy-leaved white flower with petals like rabbit-ears, wild strawberries still green, scentless violets, anemones, two kinds of orchises, primroses, the heckberry very lovely, the crab coming out as a low shrub.

Above the wood I sat on the grass and stared across Blaswater: too sublime a vista to accord with thoughts of drowning! And yet drowned the boy was, and how many thousands before him? The water blue now, as hard looking as sapphire. On the return I met an old man, driving a very large beautiful cow with two sticks. Down again into the valley, green with youth and hope.

13th May.

Miss Bainbridge arrived today, with her maid Pamela and her coachman – he slept in the coach. George has new-painted his own bedroom walls, and given it over to Miss B. to share with her companion, whilst he has had Harry put together a cot-bed inside the church, over the organ. I was not disarranged from my own sleeping arrangements, and, God be thanked, news of her arrival reached the house an hour before she did, for her coach was spotted on the north road where it had stopped with a wheel in a rut. So I had time to ready myself, and was smiling and ready when she came in, and embraced her (I said) as the sister she would soon become.

She smiled in return, and we all took a late luncheon together around the table, Miss B. the while scanning the smallness of the chamber with poorly concealed contempt. She raised her veil for lunch and I strove not to stare at her face; yet the pockmarks are *so* deep and puckered it is very hard not to. The constellation is a cluster, no mere plow or Orion's belt. Yet it is not her fault she caught the smallpox, and (as G. hath told me, once) our fortune too, for had she kept her youthful beauty she would not be settling for a marriage with a mere vicar. And I pray to God my heart is not poxed itself, with avarice, to think of what her money will do – for George, and his preferment in the South.

She made conversation with G. mostly, and listened to his replies with her head aslant. She begged him to meditate aloud upon the terms of the Grace he had read before we ate, and he did so. Finally she turned to me, and asked of my news.

I was distracted at this point, alas, for I had noticed one new thing I never noticed in London. Her left eye is white and blind from the pox (as I knew before), and only her green-hued right has any vision; but sitting so close as I was I saw for the first time that one of the pockmarks upon the left eyeball was a little outward protrusion of the corneal matter, like a tiny colourless nipple. When she turned her eyes towards me, this white, bobbled globe swivelled as the good eye did, and the fact of this – for some reason, tho what I cannot fathom – filled me with dread.

I replied, speaking too rapidly, of the stellar news – how stargazers had come to the district from far away as Potsdam and Callais, to observe the strange lights in the sky; and how the moon's own circle betrayed flickers and glimmers of short lived light inside its crescent, where the silver arc hems the darkness. Miss B. was bored by such talk, and altered the topic with a suddenness that rebuked me.

14th

Mrs Gill being (she said) too bentbacked for the chore, I assisted her in hanging out the linen. A fine and sunny day;

Miss B. sat upon the lawn and read. George kissed her hand a thousand times if he did it once.

That night I slept uneasy, and dreamy a vivid dream. First a will-o-wisp came into my bedchamber, and flew about, swinging shadows dizzy and rapid from my sideboard and shelf and the hook upon which my dress depend. It came close, and the light was fierce and hurt my eyes, but before I shut them I saw it to be a globe of white light, a perfect spherical pebble of brightness, save for one puckered protrusion upon it. I almost cried aloud, but then it was gone and I could hear a lapping, sucking sort of noise; so that I looked down to see that Blaswater had burst all banks and flooded my room, the water lapping at my bed and making it into a boat. I was concerned at once for the others in the house – for if the water had come up to the level of my chamber, then the downstairs must be fully submerged. I sat up, and saw the ghost of the boy standing, like Jesus, upon the water. 'Why are you come?' I asked him. 'To call you to affirm,' he replied, and opened his arms. 'Are you the ghost of the boy who drowned?' I demanded. 'How could you be he, if I saw you before the lad perished? Come, tell me: *are* you the ghost of the boy who drowned?' 'Cynthia,' he replied, and it shivered me to think he knew my name. 'Could I ever be that boy's ghost? Was he *my* ghost? How can we tell, without the ordered progression of time, and time the product of cause, and cause of geometry. Saint Peter holds the door open, and perforce the waters will flow through. But once you have stepped inside, let he and I force the door back to its frame, sealed tight, and we will be safe.' Then the waters lapped higher and covered the bed, and they were so cold as they touched my skin that I awoke. I discovered I had disgraced myself in my sleep, and caused my bedcloathes to become wet, and I was ashamed. I pulled off the sheet and laid it out flat from the shelf to dry it; and slept on the bare mattress, with straw-spikes poking through the weave, and wrapped myself in a blanket.

16th May.

I mark this day with a white stone.

George took Miss B. to the coast – or, rather, she took him, for it was her coach they rode in – so she could lay her one eye upon the Irish Sea, a sight she had never beheld. I alone in the house, and happy to be so. At ten Eliza comes, and no surprise was ever sweeter in my life.

We walked arm in arm around the church three times, in the sunlight, and she told me of her days. Her husband (she says) is an amateur observer of the night sky, and possesses a telescope he himself commissioned from a Liverpool glass maker. He keeps an office in Broughton West from where he administers His Majesty's levies and taxes, and this has a roof upon which he often observes the heavens. He has been in a veritable hog's heaven of happiness (she said) that so many astronomers are come from London and abroad to watch the skies over Blaswater and the other lakes. I clenched my fist and shook it at the thought of her husband, and asked her how she could bear his embraces? How endure to have him kiss her face? She laughed, and shushed me and called me greenhorn, but with tenderness.

We came inside, and retired to my chamber, where we embraced upon my bed such that her clever fingers worked me. She rose from the bed to retrieve something from her bag, and the shadows of daylight through the draw curtain fell upon her nakedness in stripes. O, how beautiful she was! The mother tigress, and I her willing prey. From her bag she brought out a short truncheon of mahogany wood. 'Do you know what this is?' she asked, and I confessing ignorance she told me: her husband's office had been furnished with a tallboy bench, upon which petitioners and visitors might sit, but that it had grown rotten with woodworm and he had it sold for firewood. 'This was one of the ornaments upon the top,' she said, turning it over in her hand: a foot long, the shape of an apothecary's bottle, the solid wood smooth and varnished. 'And I saved it from the lumber. Can you think what use I wish you to put it?'

'I would hate such a breach in my flesh,' I told her, clasping her as she lay again beside me. 'It calls to mind the spear being thrust into the side of Christ.' I trembled a little, afeared to have made so blasphemous a comparison, but Eliza laughed and kissed my face.

'Nor should I do anything to damage you, sweet girl,' she told me. 'To deny your husband-to-be his rights to your veil. But I am an old goodwife and mother, and you can do me no harm, and rather much pleasure, by doing as I ask.'

And so I did, holding the truncheon firm and working it as Eliza bade me, and kissing her too where she instructed, soon she cried very loud and fell into a sort of swoon. So I clasped her and she kissed me again, and kissed my bosom, and kissed my whole skin, until I too cried aloud.

We dozed, and afterwards dressed, and walked out into the sunshine. But so contrary and warped is my soul that the thought of her words were a worm in the bud of my happiness. 'Why must you talk of my husband to be?' I demanded of her.

'It is the world's way,' she said. And then, drawing her arm thro mine, she added: 'and it has consolations. Children are a joy.'

'No man will marry me,' I said, in gloomy mood. 'Have you not heard? I am the mad girl from London.'

'My nephew does not regard you in that light,' she teazed.

She meant it kindly, I daresay, but it soured my mood. We stopped in an ingle along the way, and watched the sunlight shift intricately upon the waters of Blaswater. The thought of the drowned lad came to me, and I leaned in and begged Eliza's pardon, and wept into her shoulder. She soothed me, and soon I was placated.

I asked if she had heard of the drowned boy. She had. I told her then that I had seen his ghost, 'yet, I fear me, I saw him before he drowned. How could that be?'

She did not mock me for this, but sat serious and thoughtful. 'I have heard of such things. Know ye the stories of Zoroaster, the Eastern mage? Precedent visions of those who would later day. He met himself, they say, in a garden in Babylonia – five thousand years ago!'

This thrilled me, the vista opening of great time and exotic locale. 'And what did he say? Upon meeting himself?'

'My goose!' said Eliza, drawing me closer. 'How avid you are for such stories! As I heard it, the mage met his own self, and greeted him fearfully. And his own self said to him, why hast thou not affirmed what thou art sent here to affirm? And so he vanished. But Zoroaster died in fire, a holy fire, and now the Brahmins – or the Parsees, I forget – worship him as god. What *is* it, sweet girl?'

She asked because I was trembling suddenly, like a fever-stricken thing, and she embraced me hard to squeeze the shudders away. I told her then what it was the ghost lad had told me, and she looked very serious and contemplative.

'Perhaps,' she said, 'he was no ghost. Perhaps he was a visitor from heaven?'

'He looked no angel,' I told her. 'But only a beggarly boy.'

'Do not think me a heretic, I beg you yet shall I tell you what the Hamiltonians believe about the crucifixion of Christ.'

'Who?'

'They are a zealous group based in Edinburgh, but with

many followers in the north country. They say Christ was but thirteen years old when he was crucified – and not thirty-three, as the Church of the Nation doth affirm.'

This interested me much, and she explained the beliefs. For thirteen is a magic age in the life of Jews, where they hold a special service to celebrate, as is well-enough known; and the gospel account of Jesus' ministry is hard to reconcile with the fullness of thirty-three years, it seeming to leap from babyhood and the prodigy infant who amazed the rabbis in the temple straight to the end years. 'And where,' she asked me, 'did those twenty years go, from thirteen to thirty-three? God made man and walking about the world! What did he spend his time doing? Carpentry? It is monstrous to think of it. Very God in the form of a human being – how could he dawdle so, and undertake no deeds? No, say no, say rather: God moved from boy to man at thirteen, and this consummation marked the time of his death and resurrection. For ceasing to be a boy and becoming a man is a form of death and resurrection; and Christ made literal what was symbolical before.' These and many other proof she furnished me with, and for a while I wept anew at the thought of that terrible day, the first ever Good Friday – not a grown man spread-eagled upon the cross, but a mere boy!

'Yet does not Luke chapter 3 state that Jesus was thirty when he began his ministry?'

She nodded, with a reverential expression on her face. 'Luke 3:23: he began to be about thirty years of age when he started to preach. Began to be – which means, clearly, was not yet. And the Hebrew for thirteen and for thirty are very close, being letters rather than numbers. Say, then, that Luke wrote: he began to be about thirteen, and the scribes altered it or misread it, and the translators corrected it – who knows?'

'Would so many people follow a mere boy?'

'No mere boy – God in flesh!'

'But the crucifixion took place under Pontius Pilate – and surely he did not become prefect of Judea until – AD 30, or some such date?'

'The year 26, as Josephus confirms. Yet what but sentiment attaches us to the idea that Christ was born at nought AD? We know only that he was born under the reign of Tiberius, and that some census of edict recalled the Jews to their homeland. But there was such an edict – in AD 19, when Jews were expelled from Sicily by the thousands. And elsewhere in the Empire too – Tiberius expelled the Egyptians from Rome, and as they returned to Egypt they displaced Jews who had settled there. We know the Divine Family had connections in Egypt; perchance this was the time they came to Bethlehem. To Egypt they returned, when Christ was an infant; and he returns to Jerusalem for his bar mitzvah at the age of thirteen. It could be he was crucified upon his thirteenth birthday itself!'

I shuddered. 'Were the Romans so barbarous – to torture children?' But I knew the answer to my own question, for truly I have read enough in the Latin histories. 'But to think of Christ – unbearded? A mere boy?'

'A boy, nothing mere.' She looked, abstractly, at the waters of Blaswater. 'He is the lamb of God, not the sheep of God, is he not?

I pondered this as we walked. There seemed some strange potency in the notion, for all that it is (I daresay) heretical. I resolve never to mention it to George, who would rebuke me, as ever, with 'Cynthia! Cynthia!' in sorrow. Yet why should we picture Christ as a man, bestially bearded and full of the ripeness of maleness? Is it not more perfect – more perfectly fitted to the universality of the saviour's mission – that he stand, as the thirteen-year-old boy may, before (as the antients say) his beard had come in, as both male and female in beauty? Or do you assert that Christ came to save men only, and leave women to their damnation? I vow: to explore this more carefully. Perhaps I shall surrender my present Latin, and return as G. has sometimes bid me to the Patristic writing. For in them may be some clew.

Home again, we embraced once more, with such purity and passion and bliss as I cannot frame in words. After I, timid, showed Eliza my precious print of the Tyger poem – pressed it upon her as a gift, for I have the lyric in my head. She reluctant was eventually moved by my importuning. I told her she was the tyger in a woman's hide of which Shaks. spoke, and how I loved the grace and power of her beauty. She kissed me, as a bridegroom might, and when the men returned we were sat drinking tea as respectable as any old maids. As I sit a-writing, by candlelight and alone in my room, I believe myself happier than I have ever been.

17th May:

Church. Oh I am loved, surely I am loved, I must be loved – how can it be otherwise? The Holy Spirit is fed by the love aura that surrounds me.

18th May.

I wrote Eliza a long letter today, and paid a boy called Little Joe, who works upon a farm, twopenny to carry it – for I know he cannot read. I have studied such books are here, or in the church sacristy, on the matter of the age at which Christ was crucified. Eliza is quite correct that nowhere in the Gospels nor, I believe, in the early Patristic writings of the Church, is that age specified. It is likely he was born before the death of Herod (Ἡρῴδης), but I can find no warrant that this must refer to the Great. In Matthew it says "When he arose, he took the young child and his mother by night, and departed into

Egypt: And was there until the death of Herod: that it might be fulfilled which was spoken of the Lord by the prophet, saying, Out of Egypt have I called my son." Yet did Herod Archelaus (which name also means 'great ruler' or 'mighty') not die until AD XVIII. If Christ were an infant at that date, he could only have been born perhap in AD XVII. And Archelaus is mentioned by name in Matthew 2:22. This Herod it was, not his father, who murdered all the baby children of the Hasmoneans. And the Census of Quirinius take place during Herod Archelaus' life? As for the Crucifixion, it happened during the time of Pontius Pilate, who assumed his duties in ADXXVI; and it occurred upon the Friday before Passover, which – according to Reverend Ritson's researches – must mean one of three dates: AD XXVII, XXX or XXXIII. Were he born before the death of Herod Archelaus in AD XVII then might he truly have been XIII years of age in AD XXX and crucified as such.

The more I read the more convinced I become and wonder only that the Church has not countenanced the idea. What, save habit and ritual, fixes our minds upon a hairy Christ in his middle-age upon the cross? Is there not more pathos, as well as beauty, in the beardless visage of a thirteener.

19th May.

A letter from my beauteous tiger returned to me this day, tho it be but cool in tone yet it is not actively rebuking or dismissive. It is, in truth, short and mere courteous. I try to rowze spirits but am gloomed nonetheless. O glimmering spirits! Be not so easily quenched!

Today also a parcel from Miss Bainbridge, of Cottle's new Poems, from London (tho printed in Bristol, yet sold out of Paternoster Row). This is a kindness of her, and signals an attempt to heal the breech between us, I know; and G. is excessively pleased to have this token, and embraced me. 'When we are sealed in holy matrimony and you two are sisters,' he saieth, 'how happy a family shall we be then!'

1st June.

I mark this day with a white stone.

I so mark this year, my whole life! To be loved to be loved. Eliza called, and tho G. was closeted with the printer Hebblethwaite (a good man, if gruff in manner) over the price of printing his sermons, yet did they two walk out for fresh air and my love and I thus gifted a precious hour together. We lay together upon my bed. She told me her letter of last week was for appearance sake, and that she cannot and I should not dare expose our connexion to the rebuke – and sanction – of public mores. We must keep it secret. 'My boys will return from school in the summer,' she warned. I care not for the summer to come, I only care for the summer in her arms.

G. marked the levity of my spirits; he thinks it occasioned by his betrothed's gift to me, and I flirted with the devil's falsehood by not correcting him. He spoke also of Eliza, but only to say that he suspects Mr Jones, her nephew, of aiming his heart at my hand in marriage. I pooh-poohed this, but the look he gave me made me to wonder if he suspects that of being the cause of my giddy spirits.

At night, by candle, writing: a fox is on the roof – too large, I think, for a squirrel or mouse, and pittering its steps along the length, pausing, and running back.

The sound of the candle flame, like a tiny banner fluttering in a distant wind, the only other noise to stain the perfection of the night's silence. The candle sheds many perfect pearls of wax into its dish.

5ᵗʰ J[une].

White stone, for tasting the bliss of my E.

14ᵗʰ June

Sabbath. Today G. preached a strange sermon, coughing much as he proceeded.

He began with the text from the VIIIth Psalm: 'When I consider thy heavens, the work of thy fingers, the moon and the stars, which thou hast ordained; What is man, that thou art mindful of him?' and spake of how man holds a special place in the divine affections. But then he said (and it caused the congregation to stir somewhat in their seats) that there had been many strange sights in the night sky, and that astronomers had come to our lakes from as far abroad as Greenwich and Hanover to observe these. What did they portend, these lamps in the heavens? Were there lunarian beings, lighting fireworks for our benefit? Did men and women of alien form throng the spaces between the worlds? If so, he said, then we can be sure only of one thing – not their form, nor the number of legs they possessed, nor the hue of their skin, but only this: that in the blood of Christ they are redeemed, or not at all.

Afterwards, that very afternoon, he confessed he had borrowed money from Miss Bane to purchase a telescope, and watch the heavens. He spoke with great animation about conversations he had shared with Mr Powser of Greenwich, who was conversing with Hebbelthwaite to produce Glories of the Starry Heavens, observd from the Lakes of Northern England. A fellow called Paul Smith, a German despite his plain name, had come hither and was lodging in Alfield; and there were half a dozen others. At first I thought G. strange in his *enthusiasmus*, but after I bethought me how wrapt up in myself I have been, not to have noticed. I resolved to accompany my brother upon the next gazing at stars – tomorrow night.

15ᵗʰ June.

An ordinary day succeeded by an extraordinary night. At G.'s invitation, a dozen men came to the cottage, most in carts or carriages to carry their observing gear. It was too many to entertain indoors, but luckily they were keen only to stay without and watch the heavens; and we heated some shrub in a pan and served it. Muffled in every scarf I loitered to peer through their devices, and saw the terrain of the moon in shocking detail. The Westmoreland Lunarians, one wagg called them; and I soon grew cold and came in again to sit by the fire.

Smith spoke to me: a lean, intelligent-looking man. He said his name the Deutzcher way as *Powell*, and kissed my hand, but coolly, not rapaciously as some do. Paul Rilke Schmidtt from Hanover. There was also a Mr Sales from Yorkshire, with the largest telescope of all the group.

I dozed a while, and then heard shouting and jubilation, and came out in a rush. The sky was filled with turning stars, shining with powdery white and yellow and some few with cooler, algae greens. Miniature comets, cometinas or cometicules perhaps, hurried left to right and right to left. Soon enough all the stars, shining with the light of a summer dusk, turned browner and redder and began to move in a mighty swirl, as birds do that flock before leaving English skies for the winter. And then they vanished, and we were left with the white nailheads of our own fixed stars.

How we shouted and hallooed at this extraordinary show! Mr Powser hurried indoors to write down an account and make sketches by the lamplight within. Mr Sales chattered excitedly to me, unconscious in his grinning at my reply, or lack thereof. Only Mr Schmidtt was calm in the teeth of this. 'Some form of meteoric storm, characterised by luminiferous energy,' my brother pronounced. 'And akin to the Northern Lights, perhaps?' I grew tyred, and went to bed, being woken from time to time by the excited chatter of the men downstairs, but always falling asleep again.

16th June.

Again the astronomers gathered upon the sward between our house and the church to watch the skies, but tonight there was no repeat of the splendours of the previous night. My brother out with them, the cold air agitating his chest and causing him to cough as regular as a grandfather clock; the sound muffled somewhat by the distance.

17th.

Again tonight. It grows tiresome, and interrupts my sleep.

19th.

News comes today that the King of France has died, Louis Seventeen, and he not yet 13 years of age. I, speaking with Herr Smith, who has again come to observe with the others, asked whether he thought the heavenly display we saw portended such a thing? He thinks not, since the French monarch's death preceded that date by some days, and that the lights could not have been seen in France – indeed, London itself was too far south to have seen them. 'Only here, Madam,' he said, and looked at me most close and intense. He is a queer fellow, and chill, but I do not mislike him.

28th Sabbath.

This afternoon I read again the Gospel accounts of Jesus' ministry, picturing not a grown and bearded old-fellow but a beauteous faced thirteen year old boy. What a revelation and freshness this exercise brings to scripture! The rightness of it shines through the chapters – surely, surely it is the truth.

30th June.

Dreadful news today. Mr Sales, one of the astronomical men – raised in Leeds in Yorkshire, and visiting only, has drowned in the Blaswater. Drowned! The 'Lunarians' as they facetiously style themselves, had moved the sights of their observations up the high hill, and I for one glad that the hubbub has been quieted upon our lawn. But it seems this Sales took into his head the fancy that he must take a telescope out upon the lake – at night! in the coaldark, and all alone. 'As to why,' G. says, 'he thought he would spy better *down there* than on the hill's summit, I do not know.' But he came not back, and the morrow his floated boat came back overturned, his equipment and himself nowhere to be seen. It is very sad, and Mr Powser of Greenwich, who esteemed Sales much, wears a black armband.

I should be sad, yet I cannot be; for this afternoon – and

after a dismal stretch alone – I again saw my Eliza, and we had some half hour alone together. My heart swoops and soars as did the luminiferous borealis we observed upon the midmonth!

She again begged me to discretion, and pushed me away as I clung to her for she heard footsteps outside the door. 'If only we be discrete my pretty thing,' she whispered, 'we may continue to commune with one another!' She said we will be apart for the summer, but I refuse to countenance such a gulph. I have told her I shall press my brother to take me to the sea-side, and will call. She, shook her head and chucked my cheek.

2ⁿᵈ J[uly].

They have searched the lake and found no body. Mrs Gill says that motion of wind and waves casts flotsam upon the western and southern shores, but nothing had appeared. It seems poor Mr Sales is at the profoundest bottom of the waters. I exchanged no more five words with him, yet am I sad at his loss.

6ᵗʰ.

Strange news – Sales has returned. He was discovered wandering in Ambleside on Friday last, and indeed arrested for affronting the peace (on account of being naked, I believe; altho G. spares my ears such words, thinking me innocent). He has been released and returned to his lodgings in Alfield yesterday, and G., who has spoke with Mr Powser, passes on his account. The magistrate believes him to have been attacked by footpads and perhaps locked in a barn or stronghouse. His tale, it seems, is full of fancy, as he was hopped into the sky like a fish on a gleaming line, and sojourned naked in a brass-walled room, and fled from thence into a glass tank or chamber. He is much distracted, they say, and the doctor has given him opium to calm his nerves.

10th

My spirits are crushed – and shall never be restor'd. The devils are about me, in flashing lights and flickers of hellish luminescence. I copy these lines from Cottle's Poems, for they speak to my life:

> *Whilst hidden fires her frantic bosom scorch*
> *Whilst to her eyes the Furies hold their torch;*
> *Adjust each feature with satanic grace*
> *And dance their orgies round her kindred face.*

Three

I write some months after, and in a calmer state, to attempt to recall what passed on the evening of the 30th June, and in the weeks and months that followed. Despair has been my constant companion, my lady's maid, such that I am quite accustomed to her. The hand in which I writ my last entry, above, speaks clear enough of my agitation and grief – so sudden and so ghastly I pray I may nevermore experience it.

The viewing upon the hill being indifferent, G. hosted the largest party of the Westmoreland Lunarians of all upon our lawn again, and hung lanterns from the trees behind the house. This was in part to celebrate the miraculous return of Mr Sales, tho' he being as yet indisposed from his experience – whatever it may have been – did not attend. Yet many people came and lined up their telescopes in a long row between our modest cottage and the church. The atmosphere was festive, and Eliza came, with her nephew. He was tiresome in his attentions to me, tho I flatter myself I responded courteous enough; and his face was apple red with the cold, or with the passion he felt for me – it seemeth to me now so remote a thing, I can record it here with equanimity. It was Tuesday June 30th, a date I shall not soon forget.

I sought some moments – only! – to be alone with Eliza,

but people were in and out of the house, and there was much commotion. And, *mirabile!*, there were more lights to be seen in the sky, quite different to the ones spied before. These were globular, and misty, and coalesced and deliquesced in green-ish, white-ish pulses lasting perhaps a minute. The oddity of them was the impossibility of determining whether they were large objects far away, or smaller objects closer by. A reddish tint appeared in one, and the gathered astronomers lowed like cows with admiration at this thing.

This, at least, drew everyone out into the night air, and I, catching Eliza by the elbow, kept her in the parlour. 'I must speak with you,' I told her; 'and it must be in camera.' She was by no means willing, and hushed me, and shooed me away. 'There are too many people,' she said. 'We cannot be seen together.' 'And if we are seen?' I teazed her. 'We are friends, and perhaps exchange an embrace and a kiss as chaste as any two sisters might?' 'Chastity is not the currency of our kisses,' she replied, yet I thought I saw in her eyes a kindling of light, so I drew her further in – and she did not break away – and kissed, and my heart sped faster than a sea under a storm-blast. I kissed her again and could hear the excited chatter of the men outside; and the thought of them outward, and my love and I inward, a sense of perfect well-being, of perfect affirmation of the cosmos, grew in my body. Never have I, I know, and never again will I, I believe, have this sensation. It was the perfection of human life, achieved only in a moment.

Eliza was wearing a coat against the chill of the summer night, but not a bolster, or scarf, and I unbuttoned its front and moved my hands upon her. She again told me to desist, but in weak tones, for she was also excited – my hand felt the motion of her heart, separated by me by warm skin only, and no dissimulation. I pressed us into the coign of the parlour, behind the door; she being taller than I, and of course older, yet did not push me away as I did so. With my other hand I felt my way below her belly. She, the while, bent her head down and bit into the cloth that covered my shoulder, for to quiet her own voice.

From the side of my eye I caught a glimpse of something, and turned my head a little, and saw Mrs Gill. She was standing on the far side of the parlour, and gawping direct at us. I had forgot she was even in the cottage, for her usual way was to pass home at dusk; yet my brother had hired her to help with the many astronomers without, and she was bustling. I stared at her, and she stared at me, and the moment sank through my innards like a stone through treacle. In a moment, like a fox spotted in the long grass, she was gone. I disengaged myself from Eliza, she saying 'what, my coddle? what is it? what?' the while. 'We were observed,' I whispered, and she stiffened.

By the time she had buttoned again her coat Mrs Gill was back at the parlour door, and my brother behind her, he pushing through and glowering at me in evident frenzy and coughing a long string of shallow coughs, as if unable to catch his breath.

'How now, brother dear?' I asked, but my voice betrayed me.

'Mrs Jones,' said my brother. 'I tender my apologies, and the shame of my family upon the altar of your affronted modesty.'

'George!' I said, sharply.

'No, Cynthia,' he cried, veritably a shout. 'It is too much – your wickedness has overcome you again.' He lost the end of this sentence in a lengthy coughing fit, that turned his visage scarlet.

'I hardly know what to say,' said Eliza. 'I am – in a shocked state.'

'O my dear Mrs Jones!' said G.

'I had not known,' said Eliza, drawing herself away, 'that your sister's affections tended so.'

'Eliza!' I begged. Oh, I was poleaxed. Poleaxed.

'Cynthia, I am sorry for you,' said Eliza, holding the front of her coat closed before her, and beginning – the first tears I ever saw from her face, and they crocodiles! – to weep. 'I am sorry that my sisterly affection has been so misunderstood!'

At this, all words froze in my throat. I was too startled even to cry.

'I can only say, Mrs Jones,' said my brother, leading her away, 'that this is not the first time my sister's unnatural appetites have imposed themselves on another. The last time, she swore to me she would restrain the Gomorrhean devil within her, and I trusted her – alas.'

And with this, she was gone outside.

I sat down in the parlour chair, and Mrs Gill stood across the room and glared at me. This, then, is what betrayal feels like – I had read about it so oft in poetry and tales, and processed the iteration as if I understood it. Only now did I comprehend how intimate and overwhelming a sensation it is.

After a while, George returned to and stood over me. 'I have been too forgiving, Cynthia,' he told me. 'I had convinced myself that I was dealing with my beloved sister, when all the time I have been conversing with the devil that peers through your eyes. This shall no longer stand. It shall no longer stand – I must find a way to make your spirit Lot, that it flee before the cities of the plain are turned to salt by a wrathful God.'

I stood up. I was a-tremble, but not much; and the thing that most appeared to me as I took my feet was an unnatural calmness. Only one thought occupied my mind. Eliza and her nephew had come in a small gig, drawn by a pony. The boy would have unharnessed the beast and put a blanket upon it and perhaps let it to chow on the grass by the road; and therefore it would be a little time before the mount was reinserted between the rods and the gig made ready. Eliza would demand it upon some pretext of feeling a sudden indisposition, but she would yet be there, at the side of the road. And I thought: if I run straight out, and straight to her, I could speak to her. And if I spake, she would listen. And – I know not, my memory is not exact, perhaps I fancied: the two of us fleeing together, leaving the Lakes, perhaps leaving England altogether – walking all the way to the snow at the top of the world and living in a palace made of ice.

I pushed past George & through the door. My gaze straight ahead, I marched along the long line of telescopes, their poles all angled upwards like Romans saluting, and their attendant human observers bustling about them and not noticing me at all. I walked to the end of this weird honour guard, and down the slope towards the road. Some carriages were waiting, but hers had gone. I daresay, as I look back, that their boy had not even unharnessed their pony. Indeed, since young Mr W. was not an astronomer, they doubtless planned on staying but a little time.

O, but *this* realisation churned my soul, and plowed my heart, and made my lungs into shreds of cloth. My throat closed up, and tears prickled my eyeballs. There was a shout behind me from the men, and I had the sense of lights bursting, firework-like, above my head. Before me was the road, and a low wall of dry stone, and then the scramble down the bracken slope to the lake edge. I was possessed of awful clarity. The lake itself was before me. I was almost preternaturally aware of the body of water, in shape like a great serpent, or worm – a dragon, it struck me, then: the wavelets on its back scales, and the steep valley walls meeting below its great fluid belly. I cannot say for certain that this beast rouzed itself and called me over; but I did feel a great force compelling me. My shadow split itself in four and danced starwise about me in the wizard light. I stumbled into motion and crossed the road, and my hand was upon the wall, when a pressure caught my elbow and drew me back, as Achilles is drawn back by

47

Athena from harming Agamemnon at the commencement of the *Ilias*.

There was a coldness to the clutch of fingers upon my arm, and as I turned to look my grief turned somehow to dread within me. Of course it was he: the ghost boy, and I closer to him now than ever – tho the light that sparkled and smeared above, and my own tear-heavy eyes made the vision blearier still, so his scarred face seemed smoothed, mask-like. The touch of his hand was as palpable as any living person's.

'What do you want with me?' I called, and my voice was higher and shriller than I thought it to be.

'For you to hold to your affirmation,' he said, and half his face moved fluently as he spoke, and half was motionless. 'Go ahead. Step through the door of Saint Peter.'

I thought he meant to guide me back inside and prevent me from hurling myself into the waters. But then I saw he was pointing me on, and the thought of drowning suddenly filled my head, and fear gushed through me, and I started back. I stumbled back along the road, leaving the ghost-boy there. The sword was sheathed in my heart. I wept now, fully, and properly, and somehow I made my way up and over the grass and to the door, past star-gazers all of whom ignored my weeping, or did not notice it at all. My brother found me at last, sitting on the floor of the parlour, sobbing with a sheep-like baa-ing.

He guided me to my bed, and I lay upon it in misery, and then slept – to my own surprize. When I woke the house was empty save G. and me and I do not wish dwell upon him rebuking me again, and preaching an individual sermon on Genesis 19:29, as I wept and clutched his knees and begged him to stop – Oh, it is humiliating beyond the power of words. It was a Sunday morning, and he had to preach, which he did to his own bitter sense of shame, and certainty that Mrs Gill had spread word of my malfeasance about the whole congregation. I, of course, did not attend.

On the Monday, a closed carriage arrived and I departed therein, with G. as my grave-faced sentry. He read to me from Jeremy Taylor's Sermons the whole way, and never looked me in the eye once. He left the volume with me to peruse during my incarceration and so I have it to hand: and have thought much upon the learned divine's wisdom that *the nature of sensual pleasure is vain, empty, and unsatisfying, biggest always in expectation, and a mere vanity in tho enjoying, and leaves a sting and thorn behind it, when it goes off. Our laughing, if it be loud and high, commonly ends in a deep sigh; and all the instances of pleasure have a sting' in the tail, tho they carry beauty on the face, and sweetness on the lip.* At Wold Newton I was admitted to a certain house, and did not leave it for the remainder of that month, nor the month after, nor the one after that.

My days were prayer and meditation, and chastisement administered by the head of the house, Mr Magnoble. I know that other delinquent women were boarded in that house, tho' of course I did not meet them. He also boarded some children, and those all boys; so I was perforce confined for the sake of modesty and necessity to one room. I would sometimes stand at the barréd window and watched the boys at work in Magnoble's garden, or playing at games in the fields beyond the house. The wheat was green when I arrived, but soon paled and dried, and the poppies growing dotted across like freckles on a face.

The hardest thing I had to do was write a letter to Eliza, apologising to her for affronting her in the manner I had done. Magnoble was punctilious about this task. 'Do not beg her for forgiveness,' he instructed me, 'for then she would perchance reply, and you must be allowed no correspondence from her, you know. Simply express how bitter your remorse, and commend her to the love and cleansing power of Christ. Simply abase yourself to her, in words.'

And so I did.

Her instant abandonment of me was the most crushing thing of all. There had been no hesitation, and she had thought nothing of it. It was that wolf of thought, that clasped its jaws about my tender neck and would not release it: I fretted and fretted. Did she not love me? Had she ever loved me? What had I been to her, that she might use me so? I knew she had a reputation, and might lose her sons and be banisht by her husband were her true nature to emerge, and in my more lucid moments I comprehended – tho dimly – how these circumstances might force upon her, and compel her to act in a defence-of-self, regardless of the promptings of her heart. But then the grief would move upon me again, in that inner tide governed by the motion of the heart's great, massy moon of sorrow, and I would know nothing but the agony of being abandoned by the one person I loved most dearly in the world.

I would weep, and Magnoble would look on and nod, thinking I was pricked by conscience and praying to God.

Magnoble set me tasks, that I be not idle; and these – sewing, cleaning and so on – were tedious. But of course the *taedium laboris* was the purpose. I pleaded with him to let me work with my brain, and at first he refused, believing that my will, allied to my mind, must be crushed, and that brain-labour might encourage it. But I suggested pious work, and represented the Church Fathers Latin writing, and certain Protestant Divines of the XVIth Century, whose writings have never been traduced, as my subjects. He said he would talk with my brother, and some days later returned to say that I might be allowed a few hours a day to undertake such work. I wrote to George begging him, when he next visited, to pack my books and dictionaries and also writing materials into a small trunk and bring them with him.

My brother visited twice. The first he looked greatly distrait, and tyred. I knew the expense of confining me at

Magnoble's was very great and wished only that I could console him – for my undesire to be there was surely as great as his undesire to pay this burdensome fee – but of course I could not mention it. I asked in as mild a manner as I could, and with as general a focus, how things fared in the Parish, but he directed so hostile a look at me as I knew he thought me angling for news of Eliza, and so I put my gaze to the floor and sobbed a little, and told him I had prayed to God with more fervour and earnestness since coming into Yorkshire than I ever had before. At this he began to weep too, tears being most unusual addition to *his* eyes, and we knelt together and prayed aloud, the Lord's Prayer.

Thinking to leaven the mood, I asked after Miss B.; but at this the muscles of his face contracted, like a frog's leg subjected to galvanic shock, and he shook his head. 'I released her from her promise to me,' he said, 'and begged her to feel no compunction in doing the same. She was willing to be my wife, Cynthia, but I could not proceed on even the suspicion of any untruth or impropriety. Hers is an antient name, a family whose nobility is threaded into the tapestry of English history over many centuries. I could not stain it...' He stopped, here, and drew in a great sigh. 'It is for the best. We may not comprehend the Providence of God now, in the instant; but there will be a time...' He stopped again.

At least he had brought my trunk. We parted with an embrace, but I felt sick in my torso and sad through and through after he had gone, to see how profound is his disappointment with me. But at least I now had my books.

That night I slept poorly and woke before dawn; and so I sat behind the iron rods of my window and watched the sky grow into colour, through blue and the reddish pink of a robin's feathers, and a tabby colour like a cat, and on, until it paled to white gold and cool and the day was started in its brightness. Vapour the pallor of bones pooled in the hollows, and the mist drifted in the breeze. Then the sun came and the clouds assumed the distinctness of white caulis-flower, and the mist was burned away.

I did not see the burned boy all autumn, not there, in that place. Sometimes, as I slept, I thought I felt again the chill pressure of his fingers against my arm, but when I woke I was always alone.

My shame was the only constant. I meditated long on the valence of shame and guilt, and realised as if for the first time that they are not distinct, as some hold; but rather that shame is merely the uncurtaining of the inner theatre in which guilt has always staged its drama. The disgust of others was my own disgust at myself, and these others who knew of it (as Mr Magnoble and – I presume, tho we never spoke of it – his three servants) were but mirrors to my hatred. I reconciled the misery I felt with the consciousness of desert; for I must be wicked to deserve such pain.

And the sky mackerel blue, and the air a sea in which I drown.

My work went slow, not because the Latin was hard, but because it was all I had, and I was loathe to complete it.

And so the autumn came, and I still there. Most days I kept to my room, and all days I stayed within the house, save only Sundays when I walked – accompanied by Big George, one of Magnoble's servants, as chaperon – over the fields to the church at Wold. Here I wore a veil, and shook no hands; and after returned. This, my only outing, was that to which I looked forward; and that which I pondered long after. The sights I saw, the little glimpses of people interacting (tho surreptitious was my garnering of these glimpses), the unison of voices in song. For a moment I forgot my shame, and the music and words affirmed again my soul in the world.

Let me not dwell upon this period, and in truth there is little to say – the days the same, the monotony fitting punishment to the monomania of lust – until December. On the Friday [*maginalium: December 11ᵗʰ*] my brother visited a second time, and it stabbed painfully upon my heart; for he was drawn and thin, his skin ill and his eyes drawn back into his skull like a snail's horns, and he coughed as often as he breathed, and the kerchief at his mouth came away dark. There was a blue-blackness in his lips, and his whole frame was bent over. 'You have not been in good health, I see,' I told him, and moved to embrace him – as why might not a sister embrace a brother? – except that he recoiled, and tho' afterwards wished to make amends for his flinch and come to me, yet by then was I too wounded and sorry and angry and we sat in my room on two chairs and did not speak for a long time. Eventually he asked, timid enough, if I would like to pray with him, and so we did; and this melted the ice between us a little. I asked after some neighbours in the parish, and G. answered shortly but to the point. Then I asked after the Westmoreland Lunarians, and he told me that there had been no lights in the sky at all, all through the second portion of the year – the last had appeared the night of my (and here he coughed rather than say the word), and since my departure the lights had departed too. 'There being no causal connection between those two things,' I started, but was unsure how to proceed. He told me of another drowning the lake, a young girl this time who had gone fishing on a windy day; and I commiserated, tho I knew not the lass. I asked after Mr Sales, but it seems he had removed to Leeds and G. had no news. At this he began to cough hard, and each cough dislodged a larger fellow *tussis* from his chest, until he was shaking and barking like a dog, and his face darkened. I grew alarmed and went into the hall to call Magnoble, but by the time he came G. had recovered his poise. He looked, I fear, even paler and more ill than before, but he stood and shook Magnoble's hand and left. I told him he was in no state for the journey and should rest, but he insisted, and I, recalling his involuntary flinch when I came to embrace him, felt a spurt of anger and bade him go, and if he wished it, not to come back.

This, I regret.

I wept a little after his going, but not much; and for the morrow-day Saturday I felt nothing in my breast at all. Sunday was cold and clear, and the bare branches of the trees along the road looked braided and knotted, as if a tangle were in the nature of things. For the first time at that drafty little church I felt restless and unwilling, and my heart did not go up to God. Then we returned to Magnoble's house and I ate a little tongue, bread and cheese in my room, with water. The boys were larking in the field outside, sliding down the frosted bank and whooping – from their yells I deduced that several were to be returned to their homes for Christmas, and they naturally joyed.

At this I thought to myself: I do not wish to be here. The words formed clear in my mind, with a chime-like, musical edge to them. I thought: I am what I am. Humans can make many things, but only God can make Love, from which reservoir we draw our daily rations. I had pondered this problem many times, and had told myself not to presume on the goodness of mere human appetite, tho we call it love, that people may love evil things – as, loving to murder, loving to hurt or hoard, or professing love for Satan Himself. Yet did I think this love no true love, but rather a hectic specie of enthusiasm and elation. My love for Eliza, tho, partook of the calm solidity of the sunrise air. And where love of wickedness fed the flames of hatred and the will-to-destroy, true love is known by its promptings to forgive. I asked myself the question as to whether I forgave Eliza, for not wishing to ruin herself along with me, for striving to keep her place in the world and her children.

Marvel: I did.

And once that thought sank into me, I found other thoughts. I found, as I had never found before, that I might pity her. I found it possible to imagine that she suffered, inwardly, in the worst manner because it had no vent into the world whatsoever, at what she had abjured in me. At what she had done *to* me. Christ suffered for us, but Judas suffered only for his own pride and his was the worse.

It may be that her sufferings, in the end, were worse than mine.

With this, the ghost-boy returned to me. There was a hiss, as of cloth drawn along cloth, or of the chilliest and faintest of breezes. I knew him there before I looked, and so I kept my head down, and drank some more water to clear my tongue of crumbs.

'You drowned in the lake at Blaswater,' I said. 'But when?'

'Does my face look as if wounded by water?' he scoffed.

'Why have you come?' I asked.

He was an arm-reach way, yet did I not reach out to him. At so close a position, and in such bright light, I saw all the puckers and folds on the burned side of his face with nasty exactness. It occurred to me that these were arrayed in lines, like the stripes on a tiger's back; tho the right side of his face was smooth as a girl's, and the skin thereof pure. His face, from that unspoyled side, was well favoured and beauteous. His body was thin, and cloathed in blue cloth, not fine or well-kept, yet not so ragged as (I am sure) I had thought it before.

'I have come to hear what you will affirm,' he said.

'I affirm,' I replied, 'that I wish no longer to remain here.'

He nodded at this, with a smile as might say: I understand. 'And so it is affirmed.'

This seemed to me a smugness. For all I knew (I thought), he might be one of the lads confin'd down stairs, and here to play a prank upon me. I had never in all my months in that house seen any of those boys close enough to mark whether they had scars upon their face. Yet I felt it not so, for this was no boy of our age, nor of our world neither. He lived in the lights in the sky, I thought; and perhaps it was bending down to our world from the heat of those auroræ, and into the ice by which Dante's lower Hell is characterised, that so scarred his face. For ice can scar as sharp as fire.

'Affirmed?' I repeated. 'How?'

'Affirm the thing itself,' he said.

I could feel his head, without laying my hands upon it. There was a new force inside me. I report the events that followed as plainly as I may, tho' they can hardly be accounted *plain*. But I would not you think me deranged, or hallucinating only. My experience was certainly realer than the muslin-blindfolded reality I had experienced at that house.

I reached out, tho not with hands, and at a single touch, as a musicians strikes a tuning bar to bring out a note, pure and simple. His head was a stone. Of his body I know not – save that when I spread both my arms wide, I saw nothing below the stone but air. I felt the weight and density of the stone, yet held it easily, or it held itself, I know not. Clouds passed from the sun as the bride's veil is drawn away by the groom, and the globe shadow appeared dark and clean-edged on the wall by the door. At the sight of this, my heart overflowed with joyous force.

How a head, of bone and blood, became stone I do not know; save only that both are maintained upon the same substructure or βάσις, that is, atomic molecules, each mode or kind of atom differing from each other by accident rather than substance – such difference indeed, providing the very definition of accident. And there it was: an irregular spheroid, pale where his face had been, dark behind where once had been hair.

Then the clock belowstairs chimed three, and I was startled and the globe flew from my grasp. It shot through the barred window behind me, in a great noise of broken wood and snapped iron, to which the splintering of glass was a feathery addition The stone flew up and high and into the blue, towards the horizon. I was so scared by what I had myself done I called out.

Then I rose, and looked at the window behind me. The bars had been bent as easily as sticks of liquorish, and the two at the centre had been broken and pulled from their sockets.

The stone ball flew up and fell down; afterwards there was talk of a meteor falln from heave upon a farmhouse in Wold Newton. But I knew that not, then. My heart was still brimming. I thought to myself, I do not wish to be here, and for a moment considered climbing through the window and so freeing myself. What prevented me was mere triviality: that the window faced east, and my home (I knew) west. So I turned back towards the door, knowing it to be locked and bolted, and not knowing how to open it.

The air folded before me like cloth and I was standing beside Blaswater. It happened as instantly as the words suggest, and (it being December) I wished at once I had stopped to dress in my shawl and bonnet before going. It was shivery weather, much more overcast than the sky had been in Yorkshire. The surface of the lake puckered and trembled like skin.

The sight of the lake fascinated my eyes.

I heard the sound of cartwheels rolling and grynding upon the road behind me, and turned in startlement; but there was no cart. The sound was that of hailstones falling on the metalled road, falling from a black cloud that was being shepherded through the sky by high winter winds. The hail was coming along the road like a curtain, and soon it was on me, and my chill became much more severe. The sensation of the hailstones upon my pate and shoulders was sharp as needles, and I ran to a tree for shelter. It was bare, but provided some meagre cover. Behind the forward cavalry of hailstones came a massed infantry of cold rain, and my dress was soaked in moments.

I was quite alone: a rainy winter's Sunday afternoon in mid-December. I could have made my way along the banks of the Blaswater and found the church, and the cottage, and dried myself before the fire. But I also knew how I had travelled to this place. I had travelled to this place via *clarity*. And that same clarity told me: what would my brother say? What would he do? Of course he would believe I had escaped from Magnoble's, by trickery or deceit. He would believe I had effected this release days earlier, and crossed the Pennine Mountains on foot, or having begged a ride in farmers' carts. He would rail at me, rebuke me – and return me to confinement, either at Magnoble's or elsewhere. Word would reach him, eventually, of the broken window, when Magnoble presented him with the bill for the damage caused, if not before. And what would I say to him? That I was a sorceress now, and could fly through the air in instants?

Clarity told me: my life, as it had been before, was over.

I was out from under the tree and running over the road before I had made a conscious choice. Indeed, the first I was consciously aware I was even in motion was when I hit the water and the crystal-cold bit into me. Those frigid waters were black and bitter, and I yelped and screeched like an owl in the night at the feel of it. Then I lurched forward and the cold waters touched my collar bone, and I felt as tho my heart would cease its beating at the froze shock of it. But then I lurched forward again. My shoe (only a house shoe) came away from my right foot, and chilled mud slid between my toes, as a comb moves between strands of hair. My face went under the water, and the affront of the cold intensified and then began to pass away. I had been shivering anyway, and now the cutting sensation of cold began, altho slowly, to numb.

My muscles were stiff as stale cheese, and creaked as I forced my arms to roll; but with a ponderous, childlike motion I swam away from the shore. Rain was falling all around, and in the dark grey light of the overcast afternoon the surface of the water bristled like a bear's pelt with a million wriggling filaments. I thought of my brother in the cottage, and then I thought with a pang of anxiety of his harsh consumptive cough, and no sooner did this thought emerge in my mind than the stormcloud sent a great rasping bark of thunder echoing down the valley walls, like a giant boulder rolling in avalanche. I thought of his tears when he discovered my death, and the rain increased in intensity and the filaments that emerged in constant supply as they evanished upon the water's surface thickened and rose. I thought of his secret relief, and the rain began to ease, and then – with a second great scraping noise of thunder – disappear altogether.

I felt as tho I had swum a great age, but I am not a practised bather and my arms worked reluctantly and with aches in both shoulders. I turned, and saw the shore not so distant as I had hoped. At any rate, I bethought myself: it is deep enough here to drown myself, and I awaited the mother waters' embrace.

At this thought, with an almost theatrick showiness the cosmos confirmed my affirmation by breaking the shell of cloud and parting them to reveal the sunlight – a great marmoreal shaft of bright white light slanting from the west and rendering the surface of the waters all a-glister. I turned on my back and kicked my legs, or tried to (for they were both so deadened by the cold as I could barely feel them) and thrashed my shivering arms as best I could, to move further towards the centre of the Blaswater. The sunlight stroked the lake from west to east, and then the clouds closed again.

I pried the other shoe from my left foot, and it fell away through the mirk waters.

I looked up. Tho the rain had stopped, and I could hear no more thunder, save only the boomy sound of small waves slapping against me and one another, yet did I see lights in the clouds, and a glimmer the colour of clean white china in amongst the purple and the black. Then sparkles of brighter light in a round circlet, and daggers of red shooting out from this ring. It was a sight like unto the lights at night, at June's end, that I had seen – yet this was solitary where those had been myriad, and this was large and solid, and seemed to move with stately galleon progression skydown toward me.

It mattered not. My bones were aching so fiercely I could feel the outline of the skeleton within me. The effortful business of moving my legs against the resistance of the muslin of my dress threatened to overwhelm me, and I slipped under the surface. I closed my eyes and breathed out, but the thought of the water penetrating into every limb of my chest and choking the life from me filled me with panic – for there are contradictions in the process I was undergoing, or perhaps the truth is that the raw animal within me awoke, briefly, and struggled again for life. So I moved my legs with as much force and celerity as I could, and my head broke the waves again, and I gasped, and saw – it is hard to be certain – a basket of light, a Montgolfier device of improbable size, spilling light in rainbow glory upon the underside of the cloud and descending. My foot tangled in the leaden folds of my dress and I slipped under the waves once more.

And so I sank. There was light about me, propping itself upon columns and shafts through the granular water. Pain bunched at my ears, and then spiked so fiercely I could not prevent myself screaming – tho no sound emerged, only a bubble, and water soon rushed in. I writhed, for the pains in my chest were as tho swords were chopping through and through my lungs.

The light blazed, and I tumbled into a chamber, or out of

the lake, or perchance through into the afterlife itself. For a length of time I was unable to orient myself, for I was too busy coughing and expelling the scorching water from my lungs, and afterwards gasping and panting. When my senses returned I found myself into a dark brown cave; yet was the floor not rock but something pliable and brown and covered in stipples or nubbins that withdrew under pressure. The walls of this space were elastic, taut enough to hold, yet soft enough not to injure my knees or elbow as I rolled about. I sat up, and by forming my fingers into a blade was able to push through the barrier and feel the cold waters of the lake on the far side. Yet when I withdrew my hand, did the waters not flow in through the breach I had made, for this healed itself.

I stood up and walked to the end of my little cave; and when I turned about was not surprised to see the scorch-faced boy there, spectral or physical, ghost or real.

'I turned your head to stone,' I said. 'Or so I thought.'

'The man become rock,' returned the figure: 'and is there in that no religious *mysterium*?'

'You are here to tell me where I am.'

'You are already cognizant where you are,' said the boy. 'You have affirmed it. You only lack the contentment.'

'And why should I be content?' I retorted, suddenly hot with fury. 'She abandoned me in the downturn of a fly's wing – I loved her, and she betrayed me.'

'Did you say to her, *I love you*? The quintessence of all affirmation is those words, and that phrase. It is what God says to sustain the whole of creation. And did you utter those words to her?'

This caused me to breathe more deeply; for the answer was, of course, no – or not in those words – or not quite – or not yet – or, *no*. 'I ken what you would say,' I told the boy. 'You would say *what choice did she possess, but to abandon me*? She has a position in society, that I have not; and which I cannot gauge the pain of losing. She has her children, and would give up much, or perhaps everything, not to lose them. My reason knows this; yet my reason cannot locate happiness within it.'

'Ah, but happiness is not an ideal of reason but of imagination,' said the boy, smiling his lop-sided smile and putting his hands together. 'Peter is holding the door open, and you are within the frame of it.'

'How is it the lake water has formed this bubble, and we two within?' I asked, pressing a hand through the *membranum* again. 'What science is here?'

'You think this beast inert? A mere mass of water, combining certain atoms in a certain arrangement permitting interpenetration and motion? The natural capacities of any creature are provoked by their environs to evolve completely to their fittest form. Life, whencesoever it originates, so evolves. Or,' and he lifted a hand and wagged it at me, dismissively, 'or did you think that creatures dwelling in other worlds and other realms of the cosmos must look like *human beings*? Why should they, any more than dogs or cats look like human beings? Any more than tigers or snakes, serpents or amoeboid life does?' He shook his head slowly, turning first the clear and then the scarred portion towards me, and I bethought me (I know not why) of the moon.

'It is *alive*?' I asked.

'The puzzle,' returned the lad, 'is that anything is ever not, that anything is ever truly inert — as some things are. The history of mankind can be seen, in the large, as the realization of a veiled plan to structure forth a perfectly constituted state as the only condition in which the capacities of mankind can be fully developed, and also bring forth that external relation among states which is perfectly adequate to this end.'

'And where are we now? We are — inside its organs? Which? Its stomach, perhaps?'

'It is a body without organs,' said the boy. 'And this cell is made as a temporary structure for you and by you, tho you realise it not. Will you stay?'

'The lights,' I said, looking up (tho the ceiling was the same glum colour as the walls and floor, and nothing was visible through them). '*They* are here for *it*? They are the same people as it? Do its fellows share the same form as this… entity? Are they dragons with water for muscles?'

'Theirs is not fixed in forms after the fashion of life in your kind,' said the boy.

'Will it leave with them? Will Blaswater become a dry valley, and this water-tiger, water-dragon, swim through the heavens?'

'Or,' the boy replied, 'will the vital principle of this creature depart, unrestrained by the barriers of space and form that confine the likes of you and I? The water left behind, but inert and fluid, the entity gone away – to report, perchance, on the strange fossilised creatures that are pinned by spatiality and temporality to this conglomerated conch of a world? *I* do not know. I do not *yet* know, tho I hope to step through Saint Peter's doorway and discover, soon, very soon.'

'Saint Peter,' I said.

'In naming him I tell you only what you have already determined in your own faculty of reason, tho such may be opaque to you.'

He mentioning opacity recalled me to my circumstance. 'No, no. How is it bright enough in here for me to see?'

'You *glow*, madam,' said the boy, and laughed. I took a step towards him –

– and fell down the slope, into the air, and under the night-sky. In tumbling I hurt myself, and in truth so brewsed my wrist that I required it later to be bound up. The air all around me was chill, but clear and fresh. I got up and my dress was still heavy and wet about my limbs. I shivered in the darkness, tho even the pain of my coldness and shuddering could not prevent me being struck by the beauty of the stars above. The pricks of light were vast and distant, or small and nearby; and towards the horizon they spread into a mist that formed the Milky Way. I saw trees that brought out the sensation of remembrance, and a low long building in silhouette. Towards this I started, shuddering with the cold so fierce I feared I might drop down and die. I had no Hamletian thoughts of being or not being any more; I only wanted to be warm again. I thought of a fire in a fireplace, and a dry cloak, and so I stumbled on

The house was a mile distant, or a little less, and the nearer I got the more I recalled it – for it was Magnoble's villa, and I returned thither from Blaswater by what witchery I know not, save only that it was the same that removed me thither. I arrived at the door with bloodied feet, and tears in my eyes, and my fists made wet and feeble noise upon the wooden panels, and none heeded them, so I found a brick discarded by the side of the house and used that to hammer the door. Eventually a lantern was lit, and Magnoble's cook op'd the door, in great amazement to find me there.

I begged her to lay a fire, and this she did, as Magnoble himself rose and descended, and several of the boys too (tho he scolded them back to their beds). I was warmed, and the cook heated a little broth for me to drink, which I could hold in my right hand, tho my left was too sore to clutch a bowl.

I need not dilate upon this. I had been gone seventeen days, tho to me it seemed only some hours. I know not whence those days disappeared. The window I had broke had been mended, and Mr Magnoble had writ my brother telling him of my flight, but had received as yet no reply. I sobbed, and sought to impart to them that I had been in the lake, and yet that lake a creature from a world unlike ours in every particular, down to the composition of physical bodies, *compositum et materiam*, yet did they scowl and shake their heads.

They thought me disarranged in my wits, and soon enough I was led to my bed, where Cook (in her kindness) agreed to stay; so she muffled herself up in a great blanket, slept in the chair and I under my bedcloathes did slumber until noon the next day.

I was ill; for my feet were so scratched and battered I could not walk for three days, and my wrist must be splinted where it had broken, or been so badly sprained as to approach fracture, and the cold had entered my innards and led to fever. For a week I was nursed until I began to recover. By then, tho questioned again, I had resolved not to tell what had happened, for fear they would decide me a worse specie of mad than even before, and take drasticker action. So I said I could not recall whither I had gone, except only that it must not be far from here, and they left me alone.

I had met – I know not *what* I had met. I had experienced an experience, true or fever dream. Yet does the thought recur to me, as the scarred boy said. Say that there are beings in the heavens, inhabiting worlds, and saved (or not) by the blood of Jesus Christ from death and damnation. Say that. Yet why say that they must be like unto men and women, with two legs and two arms? And once this thought is thought, all the dogmatic rest dissolves away. For say we imagine fish-beings, or snake-beings, or what you will. Why so? All such imaginings are but translations of the forms of life with which we are familiar into unfamiliar locales. Astronomers I met whilst my brother was yet alive assure me that Venus, planet, is obscured always with clouds, most like because it is a world of oceans and seas, as the Earth is a world (mostly) of plains and mountains. Why might life on such a planet not take liquidity as its principle and form, as we take solidity? Or might it not slide *into* liquidity, as we into out cloathes? And such a being, were it to visit our world, might settle the liquid lake of Blaswater as itself. Perhaps it looked upon the land and the beings who walked there and comprehended them not. Yet sometimes people from our world would fall into the water, and the creature would receive some glimmer of communication. Who knows?

Or perhaps I dreamed the whole thing in a fever, and it is nothing but my fancy.

Into the new year, my wounds healing, I began again with my circumscribed life. But the news soon came that my beloved brother George, the prop and stay of my life, had passed to be with his Maker, from consumption of the lungs, and I alone left of all my family. This in turn led to my expulsion from Magnoble's house, for with none to pay the bills he would not retain me, mad or not. So I travelled to Leeds, and remained in that city for a week, lodging with a Mr. Kincade, and meeting with a lawyer to whom my brother's will and testament was forwarded. There being no other beneficiaries I received all, and tho it was not much yet it was enough to maintain me in modest means.

Frail still, I travelled by carriage over the Pennine Mountains and returned to the cottage, to pack up such things as I wanted, and sell such furniture as I did not. I located this journal, in the secret place I had it hid, and wrote out this account, that it not be lost.

Some in the village avoid me, and even make the symbol of the evil eye in my direction; but others are more possessed of Christian Charity, and have taken pity on my bereavement. From one of these, a certain Mrs Gregor, who had agreed to handle the sale of goods for a set fee of 18/6, from her I learned the gossip. It was meagre enough. The lights vanishing from the sky, the astronomers had all departed the region. The Church had promised a new vicar for our church, to be a young fellow called Priestley, which fact Mrs Gregor thinks comical ('fitting name to function,' she said; 'tho I hope he prove not Romish in his ministry'). I pressed her for more news.

'There was a girl drowned in the lake,' she said, and looked gravely at the floor.

'O horrible!'

'There was a fire, or so some thought, upon the water – it being late December, and night, and rainy, they could not be sure, but some in the village thought a boat in the middest had caught flame, and two men went out in a rowed-boat to help. But they found nothing, and when they returned they discovered only that Sally Cartman, wife to one of the rowers, who had stood on the jetty with her shawl tight until her man return safe, was not to be found. The next day her shawl was pulled from the water by a fisherman. It is a tragic thing.'

This news cast my spirits very low. And yet, even de profundis, it is possible to affirm. I debate with myself to write to Eliza, or not to do so. I know how she would seek to defend herself, or else how she would rebuke me for putting her in such social danger, or perhaps how she would merely shun me. Yet in knowing these things, and through them knowing her, yet still do I love her. And I hope and trust it runs not contrary to the will of God that, one day, I will meet her again, in a place other than this, in a time other than this, and be able to affirm to her face *I love you*, and so the connection will be effected.

About the Author

Adam Roberts is the author of seventeen SF novels, most recently *The Thing Itself* (Gollancz 2015) and *The Real-Town Murders* (Gollancz 2017). He has a day job, teaching English and Creative Writing at Royal Holloway, University of London, and lives in the easternmost spur of Berkshire with his wife and family.

A Selected Bibliography:

Salt (2000)
On (2001)
Stone (2002)
Gradisil (2006)
Splinter (2007)
Swiftly (2008)
Yellow Blue Tibia (2009)
New Model Army (2010)
By Light Alone (2011)
Jack Glass (2012)
Saint Rebor *collection* (2014)
Bête (2014)
The Thing Itself (2015)
The Real-Town Murders (2017)

Also from NewCon Press

Ten short stories and a poem, all previously uncollected, including two stories that have never appeared in print before and three that are original to this book. The collection opens with "What Did Tessimond Tell You", which was selected by both Gardner Dozois and Jonathan Strahan for their *Year's Best* anthologies, and builds from there.

"Roberts is not just a great sci-fi writer, he's a phenomenally interesting writer per se."
— *The Scotsman*

"*Sibilant Fricative* is undoubtedly one of the finest collections of essays that genre criticism has ever produced."
— *Jonathan McCalmont, BSFA Vector magazine*

"Erudite, entertaining, intelligent collection of essays and reviews." — *The Bristol Book Blog*

"*Titan* is one of the blandest pieces of fiction I have come across in four decades of reading novels. If the Campbell shortlist is a high-class curry restaurant of delicious, spicy and stimulating food, then *Titan* is a single slice of white bread and margarine on a white plate under the neon light of a truck drivers' café."
on Titan by Ben Bova

"Adam Roberts' strength is that he sees SF as both cerebral and playful..." — *Strange Horizons*

"Adam Roberts makes everything wonderful. If he wrote non-fiction about drying paint, I would still be the first in line to read it."
— *Jared Shurin of Pornokitsch.*

Cover art by Ben Baldwin

NewCon Press Novella Set 4: Strange Tales

Gary Gibson – Ghost Frequencies

Susan MacDonald knows she's close to perfecting a revolutionary new form of instantaneous communication, but unless she makes a breakthrough soon her project will be shut down. Do the odd sounds – snatches of random conversation and even music – that are hampering her experiments represent the presence of 'ghosts' as some claim, deliberate sabotage as suggested by others, or is there a more sinister explanation?

Ricardo Pinto – Matryoshka

Lost in Venice in the aftermath of the war, Cherenkov just wants to put his head down somewhere and sleep, but her copper hair snares his eye. She leads him to Eborius, a baroque land lost in time, and takes him on a pilgrimage across Sargasso seas in search of the Old Man, who dwells on an island where time follows its own rules. Last of his kind, the Old Man is the only being alive who may hold the answers Cherenkov craves.

Hal Duncan – The Land of Somewhere Safe

The Land of Somewhere Safe: where things go when you think, "I must put this somewhere safe," and then can never find them again. The Scruffians: street waifs Fixed by the Stamp to provide immortal slave labour. But now they've nicked the Stamp and burned down the Institute that housed it, preventing any more of their number being exploited. Hounded by occultish Nazi spies and demons, they leave the Blitz behind in search of somewhere safe to stow it…

2001: AN ODYSSEY IN WORDS
Edited by Ian Whates and Tom Hunter

An anthology of original fiction to honour the centenary of Sir Arthur C. Clarke's birth and act as a fund raiser for the Clarke Award. Every story is precisely 2001 words long.

2001 includes stories by 10 winners of the Arthur C. Clarke Award and 13 authors who have been shortlisted, as well as non-fiction by **Neil Gaiman, China Miéville** and Chair of Judges **Andrew M. Butler**.

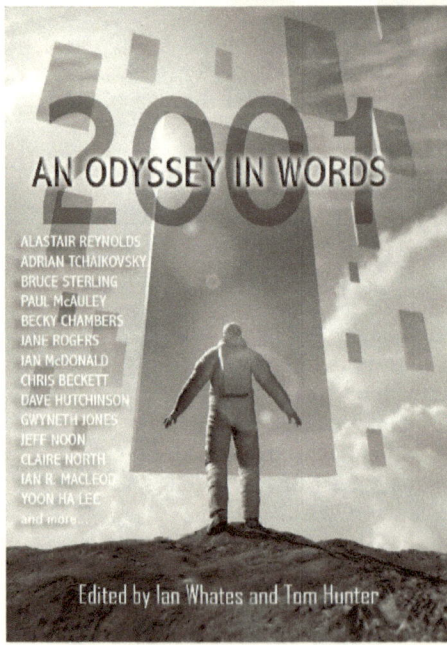

Cover art by Fangorn

Alastair Reynolds
Bruce Sterling
Gwyneth Jones
Adrian Tchaikovsky
Paul McAuley
Jane Rogers
Ian McDonald
Rachel Pollack
Chris Beckett
Jeff Noon
Colin Greenland
Becky Chambers
Claire North
Dave Hutchinson
Adam Roberts
Yoon Ha Lee
Ian R. MacLeod
Emmi Itäranta
Ian Watson
Liz Williams
& more…

Twenty-seven stories from some of the biggest names in Science Fiction, honouring one of the genre's greats by exploring the limits of imagination.

Released by NewCon Press as a paperback and limited edition hardback.